This book belongs to:

_____

Third Grade MERMAID and the Narwhals

Peter Raymundo

SCHOLASTIC PRESS/NEW YORK

Library of Congress Cataloging-in-Publication Data available

ISBN: 978-0-545-94034-4

10 9 8 7 6 5 4 3 2 1   18 19 20 21 22

Printed in China   62
First edition, February 2018
Book design by Ellen Duda and Maeve Norton

Dedicated to Dorothy, Andrew, and Feathers

My mother might be the best bedtime story reader ever! When she reads a story, it's more like a **PERFORMANCE**! And last night she was really on fire. Well, not really, because we're underwater, but the book she read had me hooked from page one—and it wasn't even a story!

She called it a "nonfiction" book—meaning it's TRUE—and it was about one of my favorite subjects of all: **NARWHALS, THE UNICORNS OF THE SEA**!

When I went to sleep, all I dreamt about was swimming around with big, graceful narwhals and their unicorn-like horns.

And that would have been **FIN-TASTIC**, if I just STAYED asleep! But halfway through the night, I woke up with an IDEA. It was for a story of my own (about narwhals, of course), and for some reason I just HAD to write it down. I just HAD to!

Mother calls this "INSPIRATION" and tries to say it's a GOOD thing. But if you ask me, inspiration is the WORST when you're trying to get to sleep!

So I've been up half the night working on this story called "Nelly the Nervous Narwhal." It's about a little narwhal who's always afraid. And when it's time for her family's migration, Nelly is so afraid of getting lost that she doesn't want to go.

I actually think the story is pretty good, but I'm still not done with it and IT'S TIME FOR SCHOOL ALREADY! So I guess I'll just have to take these pages with me and finish up in class.

Later During free time, I was concentrating on my story when—change that—I was TRYING TO concentrate on my story, but my friend Sandy kept asking me what I was working on.

Psst. Cora. What are you working on?

Sandy! For the TENTH time, I'll show you when I'm done!

Sandy looked puzzled. "Nelly? Does she go to our school?"

"She's not . . . oh, for crying out loud! Here!" I said, holding out the pages. "I'm not done. So take a quick look and give it right back."

But guess who just **HAD** to stick her snobby fins into my business?

VIVIAN SHIMMERMORE!

Yes, THE Vivian Shimmermore, who's so concerned with how she looks that she said she was "sunbeam deficient" just so her desk had the best lighting.

And even when we found out she made it up, Vivian argued that the seats had already been assigned, and she got to stay where she was.

Unfortunately, this means she's right near me. So when she asked to see my story, I'll admit I was pretty defensive.

"What? No!" I said, finding it hard to whisper. "You just want to make fun of it!"

"No, I don't!"

"I said no, Vivian."

"Well, good. I don't want to see your fake story anyway." She pouted.

That's Vivian's favorite word I guess—*fake*—which drives me crazy. Not only does she use the word incorrectly, but Vivian is easily the fakest mermaid I've ever met.

Just as I was giving the pages of my story to Sandy, Vivian shot her hand in the air and SHOUTED!

I couldn't believe it! Even mermaids can't trust sirens!

Mr. Spouter was NOT happy. And let me tell you, Mr. Spouter is one whale of a teacher (a killer whale, actually), and it is NO FUN when he gets mad at you.

Of course they were mine, but they weren't NOTES! So I figured I could just explain.

PHHH!!!"

Mr. Spouter got so mad he blew his blowhole! He can't stand it when students pass notes in class! He didn't even let me explain, and I knew what was coming next.

Whenever anyone gets caught passing notes in our class, they have to read them out loud for everyone to hear. It's usually **VERY** embarrassing.

But as I read my story about Nelly, I noticed something strange. The whole class was listening!

They only laughed at the funny parts, like they were supposed to. And no one chuckled at all when Nelly conquered her fear of the dark.

Well, almost no one!

Vivian Shimmermore started laughing and carrying on as if me reading my story was the funniest thing in the ocean.

Luckily, Mr. Spouter didn't see the humor in it.

Just seeing Vivian get clammed up like that was worth its weight in pearls. But the best part was what came next.

When I finished reading my story, the entire class erupted in **APPLAUSE**! I've never seen anything like it!

Even Mr. Spouter patted me on the back with his big flipper.

Better yet, Sandy swam back to Vivian and pointed out the glory that SHE had caused by telling on me in the first place.

Tuesday

This morning I swam to school feeling like I was riding a wave of success. Then BAM! It all came crashing down.

Cora, may I see you in my office, please?

Gulp.

As I sat in Mr. Spouter's office, my mind swam with all of the things I could have done wrong. My only defense was to confess and beg for mercy.

Mr. Spouter stared at me for a second. "Um," he said. "That's not why you're here, Cora."

"Oh. It's not? Then why AM I here?"

Mr. Spouter smiled. "Because of your story yesterday," he said. "It was surprisingly good."

"Oh! Ha ha! Well, I AM surprising!"

"Yes, you are," Mr. Spouter said. "You have a very unique . . . voice."

"Mother says I have a very LOUD voice. Is that the same thing?"

"Well, no. But it IS unique," he said. "And that's why I've nominated YOU to represent the school for the upcoming Ocean Writes Contest."

The Ocean Writes Contest?

But I can't write anything! That story was just an . . . an accident of inspiration.

"'An accident of inspiration,'" Mr. Spouter repeated. "What a great phrase! You see, Cora? You're a natural."

"But . . . but . . . I doubt . . ." I stuttered.

"There's no time for doubts, Cora. The writing entry is due next week. And I KNOW you can do it."

"Mr. Spouter," I said. "Look. I'm happy you think I'm unique and all, but I'm not a writer. I'm just . . . not. I might have lucked into one big burst of inspiration, but that doesn't mean I can do it again. I mean, there's just no way I could do it."

There's just NO WAY!

Mr. Spouter circled around me. "Cora," he said, "this contest is very prestigious. We've been looking for the right student to enter it for a long time."

Splashy!
magazine

Fins
That
GLOW!

"Well, I guess you'll just have to wait a little longer," I said, sounding confident in my lack of confidence.

"Oooookay," Mr. Spouter moaned, pulling a magazine from his desk. "Then I guess there's no use mentioning you'll get your face on the cover of *Splashy!* magazine if you win."

Hold on a second.

Why didn't you say that before?

"I didn't think it mattered." Mr. Spouter shrugged. "Besides, the real point is the writing, Cora, not getting on the cover of some magazine."

"Yeah. Sure," I said as I pictured my smiling face smack-dab on the cover of *Splashy!* "I'll do it."

Excuse me? Just a minute ago you said—

I changed my mind. I said I'll do it.

"Well, that's GREAT!" Mr. Spouter smiled from ear to ear, which is actually the ONLY way a whale can smile. "Let me go tell the other teachers," he said. Then he swam off in excitement.

Sure, Mr. Spouter was excited, but for the rest of the day, I was screaming on the inside.

Later "Aaaaaagggghh!!!" When I came home, I finally screamed on the outside. What have I done? I can't write some story for a contest!

What was I thinking?

I know EXACTLY what I was thinking! I was picturing the look on Vivian Shimmermore's face if she saw me on the cover of *Splashy!* magazine. THAT'S what I was thinking.

And I don't even really care about the magazine. All I really want is to put Vivian in her place for once. I tell you, ever since she won the Cutest Merbaby Contest years ago, Vivian's ego has been bigger than a blue whale.

The thing is, I could have won that contest, but I started crying because my diaper was wet. I didn't realize that **EVERYONE'S** diaper was wet because we're in the ocean!

But all that's a whole other story. Right now I have to win that writing contest, and I have absolutely no idea how I'm going to do it.

Too bad my pet, Salty, can't write it for me. He's the smartest shrimp I've ever met. I bet the toxic sludge that made him get so big when I first found him made his brain big, too. That's why I can never beat him in chess, or checkers, or ANYTHING!

But then there's the little fact that Salty never talks. So even though he's super-smart, I never really know what he's thinking. Of course, I've never asked him either.

Salty may not talk, but my BMFF (Best Mermaid Friend Forever), Sandy, is never at a loss for words. In fact, her talking is half the reason I'm in this mess. So I needed to call and ask her to come over.

And what better way to call her than with my brand-new **NAUTILUS SHELL PHONE**! **Model 1.658**! (I accidentally dropped my last phone and cracked the shell.)

This new phone is **SHELLFISHALICIOUS**, too! Not only is it totally the perfect shape, sometimes when I put it to my ear, I swear I can hear the ocean.

Sandy always acts like she doesn't know who I am when I call, but THIS time I'm going to disguise my voice and pretend I'm my mother calling to talk about something really serious. Hee hee!

Later Aarrggh!! Sandy knew it was me the whole time. I guess if you've known someone since preschool, you get to know what they sound like no matter what.

Well, at the very least she agreed to come over and bring our good friends Jimmy the jellyfish and Larry the sea cucumber with her.

I was sure they would think me entering the writing contest was the WORST idea ever. But boy, was I wrong!

WHAT? What does *concur* mean?

I thought you guys would convince me NOT to do it!

"Why would we do that?" Sandy said.

"Because I haven't written anything in my life!" I said.

"But what about that story you read to the class?" Sandy laughed. "Didn't you write THAT?"

"Well, yeah. I guess so." I shrugged. "But that was just . . . an accident of inspiration."

"Nothing is an accident," Larry mumbled.

"What about your diary?" Sandy asked. "You write in that pretty much every day. That helped you go from the worst speller to the best speller in the class."

"Yeah, but . . . this is totally different. For this I have to write about some topic they gave me."

"What's the topic?" Jimmy asked.

"I don't know," I said. "I haven't looked at it yet."

"Then at least you tried!" Sandy blurted.

"Cora," Larry said sternly. "This talking in circles is nonsense. Now tell us what the topic is so we can help you."

Sometimes there's just no arguing with Larry. So I grabbed the paper Mr. Spouter gave me and read it out loud.

Well, this is what it says:

"Write a story about the greatest thing you have ever done."

Wow.

"Wow is right! I haven't done anything **GREAT**!" I cried. "I'm in third grade! Great things don't happen until middle school!" At this I started feeling depressed. "I can't even think of what to write about," I said.

Then Jimmy drifted up in front of the group.

Maybe you need to think outside the box is all.

"What? What BOX?" I moaned.

"Not a real box," Larry uttered. "It's just an expression."

"Oh, it's a real box, all right," Jimmy said.

"Yes!" Larry pressed. "Just tell it already!"

"Okay, then," Jimmy said. "Everyone knows the most deadly creature in the ocean is the BOX JELLYFISH."

"It is? I didn't know that." Sandy chuckled.

"Yeah, well, now you do." Jimmy sighed, rolling his eyes. "But anyway, like most jellies, when I was younger, all I wanted to be was a fearsome box jellyfish.

"But the sad fact is, I am just a common moon jelly."

And my tentacles were too small and weak to even PRETEND to be one.

Until one day . . .

"A bunch of us were drifting past some garbage thrown in the ocean by the humans when an odd-shaped box floated down onto my head."

"Even though they laughed, for a second I actually felt like a real BOX JELLYFISH."

"Because you had a box over your head?" Sandy asked. "That's just . . . ridiculous."

"I know! It was crazy! But I floated around like that for weeks. And as I grew bigger, fitting into that little box gave me such a headache that I couldn't even think. But I couldn't take it off either, because it had molded to my head!

"So after a while I just accepted that was the best I could be: a fake box jellyfish."

"Then how'd you get out of it?" I asked.

"That's the thing." Jimmy laughed. "One day the box just felt way too small, so I pushed with all my might ... and burst right out!

"And I can tell you, once I got outside of that box, I could finally see all the things I was missing out on."

"Jimmy," I finally said. "That story is nice and all, but what does it have to do with me?"

"Well . . . nothing," Jimmy answered. "I asked if I could tell my story, and Larry said yes. So I told it."

Perhaps Jimmy has a point.

He had everything he needed to free himself but just didn't know how to do it.

"Yeah, well, I'll tell you what I know," I snapped. "I have to come up with something great to write about in the next couple days! And I'm more confused than ever!"

Thanks a lot!

wednesday

Last night I dreamt about swimming around with
a box on my head, like in Jimmy's ridiculous story!

The weird part is, I keep thinking he may be right.
Maybe I DO need to get out of my "box" and try
something new. But what?

I have only a few days left to come up with "the greatest thing I've ever done" to write about, but I don't think I'm great at anything.

I mean, I'm GOOD at things, like the 3 S's.

SINGING,

SWIMMING,

AND SPLASHING!

But I wouldn't say I'm **great** at them. I don't know. I just hope I can come up with something quick.

Later Let me just say that lunchtime in the ocean is always an event. You have the predators trying to GET lunch and the prey trying not to BE lunch. And the whole cafeteria is right next to a sunken fishing boat—I guess as a reminder that any of us could be a human's lunch.

For me, though, the biggest problem isn't a shark; it's a Shimmermore. Today at lunch I was just taking a bite of my fish and chips when I heard Vivian's unmistakably high-pitched voice behind me.

My answer is YES, Cora.

It was one of those times when you try to ignore something (or someone!) and hope it goes away—but it doesn't—and eventually you have to respond.

Vivian ran her fingers through her hair, scattering SPARKLES into my lunch! "Yes, you may write about me, of course."

"Vivian, what are you talking about?" I groaned. "Why on earth would I write about YOU?"

"Oh, don't be crabby, Cora," Vivian said. "Rumor has it you have to write about something great to win a contest, and—despite our differences—I've decided you may write about ME." Vivian paused. "As long as you share the prize," she added.

You cannot be serious.

"Of course I am," Vivian said, giving me her proudest, eyes—closed smile. "That way everyone gets what they deserve. You get to write about greatness, and I get to be on the cover of *Splashy!* magazine."

Then Vivian pulled out a pearl—encrusted mirror and started admiring herself.

It's perfect. Like me.

"Did I tell you my sisters, the Sirens, sunk FOUR ships yesterday?"

"Yes, you did," I moaned. "Twice."

The Singing Sirens. The most glamorous mermaids in the sea. I can hardly believe I used to want to be like them so badly. I mean, they barely even SWIM! They mainly lounge around in lagoons looking beautiful—which I bet is just as boring as it sounds.

Then, when a ship comes by, they use that siren song of theirs to get the sailors to crash their boats. I find this just plain mean. Yet Vivian thinks it's the greatest thing in the world, and she goes around bragging about it on a daily basis.

"Look, Vivian," I huffed. "For the contest I have to write about something great **I HAVE DONE**. Not just something great. And even if it was . . ."

Writing about you wouldn't help me at all!

Vivian's followers jumped in to defend her so quickly I actually felt kind of bad. In fact, I was going to apologize when Vivian cut me off.

"Better to write about me than some fake horned whale," Vivian said.

I almost thought she was joking.

You mean narwhals?

They aren't fake. Narwhals are real!

Vivian chuckled, causing her followers to chuckle as well. "Oh, Cora." She sighed. "I hate to tell you this, but narwhals are fake. Just like...like... other fake things!"

Ironically, Vivian was finally using the word *fake* correctly—except she was wrong. Of course narwhals are real. I mean, that's like someone thinking mermaids aren't real. Can you imagine?

"Excuse me, Vivian," Larry said politely. "Perhaps you should spend more time looking in a book rather than in a mirror." (Well, at least it started polite.) "Narwhals ARE real," he continued. "They live in the arctic waters north of here. That 'horn' you mentioned is actually a large tooth that grows through their upper lips."

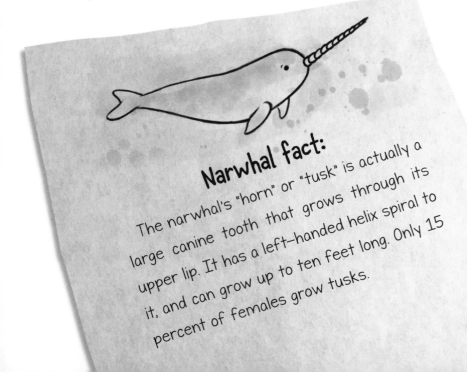

Narwhal fact:

The narwhal's "horn" or "tusk" is actually a large canine tooth that grows through its upper lip. It has a left-handed helix spiral to it, and can grow up to ten feet long. Only 15 percent of females grow tusks.

Vivian leaned into Larry's face. "And have you actually SEEN one yourself, Mr. Smarty Pants? Have you? Hmmm?"

"Well, actually, no," Larry said. "That's because sea cucumbers don't have eyes. But I assure you narwhals are indeed real."

"Ha!" Vivian laughed. Then she floated up into my face again. "You know what would be GREAT?" Vivian said. "You proving it, Cora."

Then, not knowing she had just given me what I needed, Vivian and her fishy followers swam away.

I met Larry after school, all right, near the elkhorn coral. And I have to say he was acting kind of weird.

"Shhh..." Larry whispered. "After Vivian made her comment, I sent out an unhearable call to the SSCAB."

"The who?"

The Secret Sea Cucumber Adventure Brigade," Larry said proudly. "I was just made Junior Adventurer last week." Then he showed me his badge as proof.

"That sounds pretty neat, Larry," I said. "How come you never told me about this before?"

"Because it's a SECRET," Larry answered. "That's part of the name."

"Oh. Okay. But if the call was unhearable, then how did anyone hear it?"

"Will you stop asking questions?!" Larry barked. "It can't be heard by creatures with ears. But that doesn't matter. What matters is, we have THIS!"

Suddenly, Larry pulled out a MAP! (Where he got it from, I don't know.)

N
W
E
S
Narwhal Migration
Sea Caves
Kelp Forest
Home
Narwhal fact:
Narwhals live primarily in the Arctic, migrating to ice-free waters for the summer.

"Narwhals are mysterious creatures," Larry said, "even more mysterious than the origins of this map. But thanks to the Secret Sea Cucumber Adventure Brigade, I think we have a chance."

"Well . . . aren't all of us going?" I asked.

Larry was quiet for a moment, but then he said, "Yes. We didn't want to barge into your mission, Cora. But you're right."

Friends stick together.

"All we have to do is follow that map, and I believe we can make it in time to see the narwhals before they begin migrating."

I believed we could make it, too. But there was still one little roadblock. My mother!

"No means no," Mother said when I asked to go. "You're too young to be swimming into the deep on your own. And I don't have time to go with you this weekend. Can't you do it next week?"

"No! The contest deadline is in five days!" I yelled. "And I'm NOT going by myself. Larry, Sandy, and Jimmy are coming with me!"

Mother raised an eyebrow. "And THEIR parents said yes to this?"

Actually, Sandy and Jimmy had barely said yes themselves, so I had to think quickly.

What if Salty came with us?

"Remember Salty even saved me from a gang of angry sharks," I said.

Mother knew I was right. Nothing can hurt Salty! At least nothing I know of.

"Well . . ." Mother said slowly. "Maybe if . . ."

"Oh, thank you! Thank you!" I squealed.

Now hold on, Cora. I didn't say yes.

Yes?

Oh, I knew you believed in me!

Cora. I didn't say yes.

YES?

Ha ha! There it is again! YES! YES! YES! Oh, thank you so much!

The "Yes Game" went on for some time before Mother actually said yes for real. But the point is, she did.

Now all I have to do is convince Larry's, Sandy's, and Jimmy's parents as well!

Friday

It turns out Jimmy doesn't even have parents to ask! He said I would have known this already if I'd just swum over to where he lives once or twice. But I guess that's just another example of me needing to get out of my box.

Jimmy said that jellyfish just **POP** off this **POLYP** thing they're born in, then that's it. They start flapping their little arms and make their way. I always wondered why Jimmy never came with his mom or dad anywhere. And this answers it.

As for Larry's parents, I've met them only a few times. Larry was adopted by a pair of octopuses. So he gets eight times as many hugs as most kids! Anyway, with Larry's Adventure Brigade experience, they let him go, no problem at all.

And as much as Sandy jokes around, she's been going on two— and three-day trips to visit her grandparents for YEARS! So getting her to come was easy, too.

I was sure glad all that went smoothly, and I just couldn't wait for our adventure to begin!

Saturday

If there is one thing I can say about the ocean, it's that it is **BIG**! Sandy, Salty, Larry, Jimmy, and I swam off first thing in the morning and made our way into the deep blue unknown. It was exciting and scary at the same time.

There's more out there than I could possibly imagine. And there is **DEFINITELY** more than what is on Larry's map.

Not surprisingly, we got LOST halfway through the day and had to ask for directions!

But every time we tried, the fish got so scared of Salty they swam for their lives!

Eventually, though, we came across creatures so gigantic they even made Salty look small. And get this! They were JELLYFISH, with tentacles one hundred feet long!

"They're called lion's mane jellyfish," Jimmy whispered. "They're the biggest, most impressive jellies in the world."

I'm not sure what a lion is, but I AM sure those massive tentacles were **HORRIFYING**!

"You know. Go ask for directions," I said.

"Are you kidding? Why me?"

Sandy rolled her eyes. "Because they're JEL-LY-FISH," she said, waving her arms like tentacles. "And in case you haven't noticed, YOU are a jellyfish."

"So? You think we all know one another or something?"

"Well, not when you put it like that. But can you still go do it?" Sandy asked.

"Cora," Jimmy pleaded, "those are lion's mane jellyfish. I can't just go up there and ASK FOR DIRECTIONS."

"Why not?" I shrugged.

"Because . . . oh! Because LOOK at them!" Jimmy cried. "THEY are big and important and impressive. And I'm just . . . me. I'm barely a jellyfish compared to them."

Jimmy's lack of confidence was surprising, but even more surprising was how Larry reacted to it.

"You are every bit as much of a jellyfish as anyone else!" Larry said. "And you shouldn't need a box on your head or a lion's mane to feel you're important. Do you understand me?"

"Um. I guess so," Jimmy said.

"Well, I **KNOW** so. Now you and Cora are going up there to get directions. And that's all there is to it!"

"What? Why me?" I exclaimed.

"Because it's YOUR mission," Larry said. "We have less than two days before the narwhals are gone, and our chance to see them will be lost. **Now go up there and get those directions!**"

Yes, sir!

For someone who barely has a mouth, Larry sure can open it! But I'm glad he did. Somehow, Larry barking orders like that gave Jimmy and me enough confidence to swim up into the face of danger.

Except, when the giant jellies turned around, they were nothing like we expected.

"Um. Excuse me, ma'am," Jimmy said.

By the looks on their jolly, jelly faces, you'd think these giant creatures were meeting a celebrity or something.

"Well, looky here, Herb! A teeny jelly! You must be a what? An Aurelia?"

"Yes, ma'am. I am," Jimmy said.

"Ooooweee!" Herb marveled. "Muriel, I haven't seen one of them in YEARS!"

"What's a tiny fella like yourself doing way out here?" Muriel asked.

"My friends and I are on a mission," Jimmy said, "but we're a little lost."

"Lost?" Herb seemed concerned. "Well, just tell us what you're looking for and maybe we can point you in the right direction."

He pointed at the round statue on our map.

"Sakes alive!" Muriel exclaimed. "You're more than
a little lost, little fella! You guys need to go way over
HERE." Muriel used her giant tentacle to trace a line
on our map.

"Just follow the current," she said. "But make sure you go LEFT at the sunken plane."

"Left?" Herb asked.

Yes. We floated past there ourselves. Don't you remember?

"Are you sure you're right about that, Muriel?"

"Right about what?"

"About going left," Herb said. "Sometimes you've been wrong."

"I am not WRONG!" Muriel huffed. "I'm RIGHT. You go LEFT. I'm sure of it."

"Oh, don't get your tentacles in a tangle." Herb shrugged. "Right. Left. Right. Wrong. What's the difference?"

"There's a BIG difference," Muriel said. "So go left. You got that, little fella?"

"Um. I think so," Jimmy answered. I nodded in agreement, but I felt more lost than ever.

Then, as we were swimming back to the others, Herb and Muriel called out one last piece of advice. I could barely hear it, though.

Oh. If you get to . . . Gulf Stream . . . or . . . you've gone too far!

Well, we went too far!

THIS is the Gulf Stream! It's just a current of water, but it was strong enough to knock us for a loop!

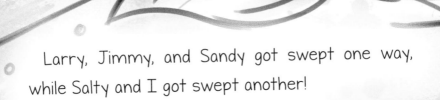

Larry, Jimmy, and Sandy got swept one way, while Salty and I got swept another!

The current was so strong, I had no idea where the others went. And I had no clue where we were either until we slammed into the Sacred Statue we were looking for.

This helped us come to a stop, but Salty knocked down a big part of the statue. As he was trying to set it back up, the craziest thing happened.

I turned around to find an army of the cutest little creatures I'd ever seen—except they were angry, which wasn't so cute.

"Sea what?" I asked, having no idea what they were.

"Sea PIGS!" the one with the crown squealed. "I am King Shinybelly!"

I chuckled. "King . . . Shinybelly," I said, trying not to laugh at his name, "my friend and I are just on our way to see the narwhal migration but . . ."

"Lies!" King Shinybelly belted. "We already saw your kind trespass here earlier, then flick sand in our faces while swimming off!"

"Look, King Shinybelly. I have no idea what you're talking about," I shot back. "But I think you better learn some manners before my giant shrimp here starts getting angry."

I thought they were going to straighten up, but all they did was laugh.

They pointed behind me. Dozens of the little sea pigs had Salty tied down with long ropes of kelp!

"Salty!" I yelled. "But how . . . ?"

"Many small things are stronger than one big thing," King Shinybelly declared. **"NOW TAKE THEM TO THE CAGE!"**

The cage was made from an old whale skeleton. And it was surprisingly effective.

Salty, I have no idea how I am going to explain this to my mom.

Sunday

Yep. I spent the entire night in a sea pig prison. When I woke up in the morning I could feel the time ticking away. *Soon*, I thought, *the narwhals will be gone, and I'll never get my chance to see them.*

"Don't I get a phone call or something?" I asked the guard.

"Quiet, prisoner!" the guard snorted. "It looks like you have visitors!"

It was Larry, Sandy, and Jimmy! Larry was crawling along with the sea pigs like they were old friends!

"KNOW them? Sea pigs and sea cucumbers are practically RELATED!" Larry said cheerily. "In fact, King Shinybelly here is an honorary SSCAB member himself!"

"Well, that's just GREAT!" I yelled. "Then maybe you can . . ."

GET ME OUT OF HERE!!!

"You know, you can just swim through the bars," King Shinybelly said. "You could have left whenever you wanted."

"You're right!" I exclaimed, slipping through the rib cage bars with ease. "The guards said I wouldn't be able to escape, so I just assumed they were right."

King Shinybelly chuckled. "It's amazing. Those who believe they can and those who believe they can't are usually both right."

Wow! That's a great phrase. Can I use that?

After we were free, Salty put the Sacred Statue back together. It was actually just a pile of large round rocks, but it looked remarkably similar to a sea pig.

This gave me a chance to update my diary.

I could hardly believe all the twists and turns we'd gone through so far, but there was another one coming!

SALTY WAS SHRINKING!

He was still big for a shrimp, but not even close to the whale-sized companion I was used to!

"Perhaps the toxic waste that enlarged him is wearing off," Larry suggested.

"Maybe," I said, "but it sure picked the wrong time to do that! We need Salty as our protection!"

At least he still has his claws.

"That's true," I agreed. "As long as he doesn't shrink any more, we should be fine."

Later After leaving the sea pigs, our next landmark was the Sea Caves. From there, we'd be able to get our first view of the narwhals.

We were behind schedule so Larry had us swim as fast as we could, which I must admit is pretty fast.

We whizzed past trenches and slopes and endless schools of fish. We even met a school of BLUEFIN TUNA that had a hard time keeping up!

But after an hour of swimming my fins off, something caught my eye.

"Hold on a second!" I hollered. "I think something's wrong!"

We all stopped. I went back a little to see what had grabbed my attention and could hardly believe it.

"Are we close?" Sandy asked. "I hope so."

"No!" I wailed, pointing at the map. "We're **FARTHER** away than we were an hour ago!"

Larry took a closer look at the map. "I'm thinking there is a lesson to be learned here," he said.

"And what lesson is that?" I moaned.

"When swimming as fast as you can, be sure you are going in the right direction," Larry said. Then he added, "Apparently we were not."

"Larry!" I yelled. "I thought you were in an adventure brigade!"

"Indeed I am," Larry replied. "I'm not sure how this happened. The only thing I can think of is . . ." He paused, thinking. "Sandy, put me down over there," he said.

"Where?" Sandy asked.

"Over there," Larry said.

Larry, which way are you pointing?

"Ahhh. You see?" Larry said. "That IS my point. I'm NOT pointing, because I have nothing to point WITH."

I took a deep breath. "Larry, I'm about to scream, so you had better start making sense fast."

"Very well," Larry said. "Sandy, please just put me down right here."

Sandy placed Larry in the sand, and he began crawling around.

"Sea cucumbers get their sense of direction by crawling," Larry said.

"Okay, but what does that mean?" I asked.

"It means that Sandy has been carrying me the whole trip, and apparently I've had absolutely no idea where I was going the entire time. Sorry."

AAAAaaaagggghhhhhh!!!

"LARRY!" I yelled. "How are we going to find the narwhals now? We're running out of time!"

"Time is indeed of the essence," Larry said calmly. "So we do need to hurry. Unfortunately, the first thing we need to do is hurry back the way we just came."

After **ANOTHER** hour of swimming back past the same tuna and trenches and slopes we passed before, we finally turned north like we should have in the first place! This time we stopped every once in a while for Larry to make sure we were going in the right direction.

I noticed the water gradually getting colder and colder. There were even small chunks of ice floating on the surface.

"Blubber?" I laughed.
"What kind of crazy coat
is made of blubber?"
"OH MY GOODNESS!"
Sandy blurted.
"What? I was joking. I just
never heard of blubber coats before is all."
"Not YOU," Sandy said. "Look at Salty!"

At first I didn't even know where to look. Salty was **TINY**! He was back to the size of an ordinary shrimp again—and he was **GLOWING**, like when I first met him.

"Well, so much for our protection," Jimmy said. "At this size, Salty could barely pinch salt."

"Yeah, but he sure is cute," Sandy added, patting Salty's little head.

Besides being smaller (and GLOWING), Salty was definitely not as strong as he used to be. Now it was me who had to protect HIM during the long journey ahead.

After what seemed like forever, we **FINALLY** arrived at the sea caves. Except there were so many of them it was hard to know which one was the right cave.

"Look for the cave with a narwhal marking," Larry instructed. "It should lead us right under the narwhal migration."

"And there's one right here!" I said. "What's going on?" But that's when I noticed something highly unusual: SPARKLES!

My mind raced! I'd seen those sparkles before!
Suddenly, I remembered what the sea pigs had
said about "my kind" flipping sand in their faces.

"But it couldn't be," I said out loud.

"Oh yes. It could be," came a familiar voice
floating up from a cave.

In fact, it is.

"Vivian Shimmermore!" I yelled. "You've been following us the whole time!"

Vivian chuckled. "Actually, I've been one fin ahead of you the whole time," she sneered. "As usual."

"How?" Jimmy asked. "We barely made it here ourselves."

"I just followed your map." She smiled. "Well, technically a COPY of your map." Vivian waved a big kelp leaf around. "I made it before you guys left . . . when Larry wasn't looking. Get it, not LOOKING! Ha ha ha ha! Oh, I crack myself up!"

"But . . . why?" I frowned. "Don't you have ships to sink or something?"

"Because I didn't want you to lie about seeing your fake horned whales," Vivian answered. "I knew they didn't exist, Cora. Just look around!"

I looked around, and she was right. There wasn't a single narwhal in sight, and we were basically where the map said they would be.

Where are they, Larry?

"Only the sea knows," Larry said. "They SHOULD be here. But if there is one thing I have learned, it's this: Just because something SHOULD be, that doesn't mean it is."

And if there's one thing I'VE learned, it's not to listen to a talking slug!

HA HA HA HA HA HA!!

Vivian just kept laughing and laughing!

Grrrrrrrr!!! Not seeing the narwhals was bad enough, but now Vivian Shimmermore, of all people, was sitting there LAUGHING IN MY FACE!

It was **JUST**

TOO

MUCH!

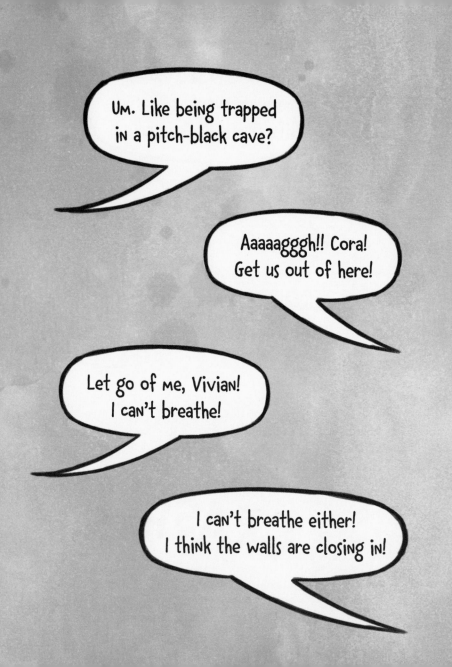

Gradually, our eyes adjusted a little to the darkness, but even with Vivian's help, I couldn't move the rocks at all.

I was starting to get scared myself when I heard a voice coming from above. It was Sandy!

Cora! Are you okay in there?

I would be, except I'm stuck in here with Vivian Shimmermore!

"Cora!" came Larry's muffled voice from outside the cave. "The rocks can't be moved, and this hole is too small for you to get out of."

"Gee, thanks," Vivian said sarcastically. "How about telling us something we don't already know?"

"You mean like the fact that I know there is another way out based on the water current moving through the cave?"

Um. Yes, but . . .

how are we going to find it?

It's totally dark in here!

First, you need to calm down, Vivian.

"I'm certain there is another entrance. You just have to go through the cave to find it," Larry added.

"BUT HOW?" Vivian yelled. "It's too DARK!"

And that's when we saw him. Salty! He came floating down from the hole like a tiny bioluminescent angelfish.

Salty may not have been the same jumbo shrimp I was used to, but when everything around you is dark, even a little bit of light is **GIGANTIC**!

Having him there made Vivian feel better. It might have just been the lighting, but I'm pretty sure Vivian had been crying in the dark.

Salty motioned for us to follow him, but Vivian was too scared to go.

"Vivian, it's going to be okay," I said, taking hold of her hand. "You just have to trust me." I was scared, too, but tried to sound as confident as I could. And thank goodness, it worked.

Now, I don't know how he did it, but somehow Salty led us all the way through that maze of a cave without stopping once. I never took my eyes off him. And Vivian never let go of my hand.

When we finally got out, Vivian and I were so happy we just lay in the sand making sand angels as we looked up at the light.

"Ahhhh! I could just lie here staring at that sun forever!" Vivian said. And that's when we saw them.

THE NARWHALS!

Vivian and I hurried up to the surface, where the narwhals were, and actually SWAM with them!

Up close, the narwhals were kind of grayish in color with fuzzy black splotches all over them. And their horns (or tusks, I should say) were much longer than I thought.

They were peaceful and beautiful and didn't seem to mind us at all. Thankfully, Sandy, Larry, and Jimmy saw them as well and came up to join us.

The narwhals were migrating, though, and before long they had to move on.

Vivian was the happiest I had ever seen her. "I can't believe we just swam with real narwhals!" She laughed.

"But I guess you have to," I said.

"Have to what?" Vivian asked.

"Have to believe it," I said. "That narwhals are real."

Vivian's expression melted back into her normal, practiced look. "Okay," she said. "You were right, and I was wrong. Are you happy? Good. Don't expect me to say it again."

"Whoa! Take it easy, Vivian," I said. "I was only joking. Besides, if it wasn't for your challenge, I may not have come out here at all. So in a way, I owe you."

Of course you do, Cora. But we can discuss that later.

Seriously. That's what Vivian said. And she wasn't even looking at me. This after I saved her from a pitch–black cave and introduced her to REAL NARWHALS! I tell you, the nerve of that girl really ruffles my scales.

Because of this, I gave Vivian the most serious stare I possibly could.

"Vivian," I said. "I do not owe you a thing."

"Well, I hate to break up the party," Larry butted in, "but don't you have to get back and write a paper about this now?"

"Oh my goodness!" I yelled. "You're right!" I grabbed Salty. Sandy took Larry, and we were on our way home. And yes, Vivian came with us.

We hurried back past the tuna and sea pigs and vast stretches of blue. Even though I was happy to be heading home, part of me knew I would miss all of this. Sure it was dangerous and scary at times, but it wouldn't have been an adventure without that.

We made it back in record time, too! Of course, it helped that we didn't get lost—twice—or put in a sea pig prison, or trapped in a cave.

So, I'm actually back home now. But it's super late, and I'm so tired from the trip I can barely keep my eyes open! Especially now that I'm lying down in my nice, soft clamshell bed.

I think . . . if I just take a small nap, I can wake up early and write my paper before school.

I'm not sure if that's the best plan or not, but I'm just . . . I'm just EXHAUSTED!

Yeah, I think if I close my eyes for just an hour or so... I'll be... just...

ZZZzzzzz

Monday

OH MY GOODNESS!!! I didn't wake up! It's time for school already, and I haven't written anything!

Relax. Breathe in. Breathe out. Maybe I can write something really quick. Let me see. If I can just come up with a decent opening line . . .

Call me Cora. No! That's too short.

It is a truth universally acknowledged that a mermaid in possession of a good voice must be . . . NOOO!

Happy mermaids are all alike, but every UNHAPPY mermaid is unhappy in her own way.

It was the best of tides. It was the worst of tides. It was the age of mermaids. It was the age of sirens . . . Aaggh! That doesn't even make sense!

NOOO!!! These beginnings are HORRIBLE! Just plain horrible!

I have to tell Mr. Spouter that I need some more time. I'm sure he'll understand.

I told Mr. Spouter all about my journey to see the narwhals and how GREAT it was, but guess what he said!

He said, "That's one whale of a tale, Cora. If even HALF of it is true, you should have written THAT down to turn in as your story."

How could he not believe me? I DID go on an adventure! I DID get trapped in a cave! And I DID see the narwhals with my own eyes, for crying out loud! If he just read my . . .

Hold on a second.

Hold. On. A. Second.

I DID write it down. **IN MY DIARY!**

Tuesday

Turning in my diary is actually the **WORST** thing I have ever done! EVER! I barely slept a wink last night knowing some STRANGER … a GROUP of strangers even, was flipping through my life for some silly contest! It's just crazy!

But what's even MORE crazy is how much I hope they like it. I mean, I can handle someone not liking a story I made up, but not liking my diary is almost like not liking me.

You know what, though? This last weekend was the greatest adventure of my life. And it really doesn't matter if anyone likes it or not. I like it. And I'm pretty sure that's all that matters.

Wednesday

Well, I have my diary back. And oh, what a difference a day makes! I have to laugh as I write this, because guess what! I was worried for nothing. People DID like my diary! What's funny is they thought it was so adventurous that I must have made part of it up.

It doesn't matter. I won **FIRST PLACE**! And here's the ribbon to prove it.

The
Ocean Writes
Contest
WINNER

The second-place story was written by a monk-fish who mainly talked about how quiet he could be. The third-place story was actually eight stories written at the same time by an octopus. Go figure.

But I guess what really set mine apart was the characters. In the letter the judges wrote to me, they said the "selfish and arrogant" character named Vivian was the perfect antagonist because she always challenged me to do more without even knowing it. (If Vivian ever saw that, I'm sure the only word she would see is *perfect*.)

The judges also loved how my friends were always there to push me forward as well. And they were right. I couldn't have won this award without all the people around me.

That's why I'm happy I could share the magazine cover with **EVERYONE** who went on our adventure . . . including Vivian.

It looks like I'm at the end of another diary, though. And to think, it all started with an accident of inspiration. I guess you never know what will happen when you swim outside your box. But I can't wait until the next time I do.

A FEW FACTS ABOUT NARWHALS:

First of all, narwhals are 100 percent real. They are medium-sized whales that live most of the year in the Arctic Ocean.

Narwhals have distinct, streamlined bodies with dark gray markings on their backs. Of course, a narwhal's most distinct feature is the large "horn" growing straight out of its

Arctic Ocean

head, just like a unicorn! Except this isn't a horn at all! It's actually a giant left tooth that spirals right through the narwhal's upper lip! Usually these are referred to as tusks.

Narwhal tusks grow in a "helix spiral" up to ten feet long!

NARWHAL VOCABULARY:

POD – a group of narwhals. Narwhals usually live in pods, or blessings, of five to ten whales, but in the summer months form groups of up to 1,000.

ARCTIC COD – species of cod fish found in icy, Arctic waters. They are a big part of the narwhal's diet.

PIGMENTATION – coloring in the skin. Narwhals are mostly white, with a splotchy gray pigmentation on their backs.

DID YOU KNOW . . .

Narwhals are incredible divers! They can swim to depths of more than 2,600 feet below the surface!

Acknowledgments

A whale-sized thanks to my literary agent, Dan Lazar. Thank you once again for the guidance you have given me, often at a moment's notice. Thanks to my amazing Scholastic family for bringing *Third Grade Mermaid* to the world. Foremost, of course, is my truly supportive and patient editor, Nancy Mercado, who understood Cora's quirky personality from the start, and the designer Maeve Norton, who helped turn Cora's pile of nearly random drawings into a visual style. Also, thanks to my Summer Reading Road Trip crew, especially Julie Amitie and Mike Oubre, for being so "fin"tastic.

Special thanks to Kellie Lewis, Ed Bloom, and Dominic Carola, who helped keep me swimming when all of the currents were against me.

Thank you Kerianne Okie, Lisa Jones, Coach Lia, Coach D, Gina Mellilo, Diann Loew, Jackie Wade, Cheryl Davis, Erin Erickson, Claire Slater, Kate Palazzolo, Lisa

Armington, Gidget Archambeau, Wendi McFarland, Linda Borick, Kimberly Coughlin, Oriana Kopec, Laurie Walsh, Shelley Rowan, the Powers family, Bok Tower Gardens, Megan George at Books-a-Million, SR Learning Headquarters, The Florida Aquarium in Tampa, and Sea Life Orlando Aquarium, for your unending waves of support and inspiration.

About the Author/Illustrator

Peter Raymundo is currently starring in his own life as an author and illustrator. Previous roles include being a Disney animator on really big movies and director of his own short films. He also has a full-time role as a husband and father. More than anything, though, Peter believes in working as hard as you can and having faith in yourself no matter your role, because everyone is a star in his or her own way.

www.ThirdGradeMermaid.com